Walt Disney's

Mowgli and Kaa the Python

First American Edition. Copyright © 1981 by Walt Disney Productions. All rights reserved under International and Pan-American Copyright Conventions. Published in the United States by Random House, Inc., New York, and simultaneously in Canada by Random House of Canada Limited, Toronto. Originally published in Denmark as MOWGLI OG SLANGEN KAA by Gutenberghus Gruppen, Copenhagen. ISBN: 0-394-85109-9 Manufactured in the United States of America

E F G H I J K L   6 7 8 9

GROLIER
BOOK CLUB EDITION

Mowgli was a boy who lived in the jungle.
The jungle was not a safe place for a boy.
But Mowgli had friends.
Bagheera the panther and
Baloo the bear loved Mowgli.
They protected him.

They protected Mowgli from
Kaa the python.

Kaa thought that Mowgli
would make a nice dinner.

They protected him from Shere Khan
the tiger.

Shere Khan thought that Mowgli
would make a tasty lunch.

Bagheera and Baloo even had to keep
Mowgli away from the monkeys.

The monkeys wanted to catch the boy.

Would any of these enemies ever help
Mowgli?

Of course not!

Yet there came a day when one of them did.

That story began one morning when
the monkeys were making fun of Mowgli.
They pointed and yelled at the boy.
"Where's your tail?" asked one.
"What a funny face you have!"
laughed another.

"Pay no attention to those monkeys," said Bagheera. "They are show-offs."

"Aren't they afraid of you and Baloo?" asked Mowgli.

"Yes," said Bagheera. "But we cannot reach them when they are in the trees."

Just then the monkeys
stopped laughing.

Here came someone who
COULD reach them.

It was Kaa!

The monkeys ran away as Kaa
slithered up the tree.

"One day Kaa will catch those
silly monkeys," said Bagheera.

"What will Kaa do to the monkeys?"
asked Mowgli.

Bagheera waved his long tail back and
forth in front of Mowgli's eyes.

Mowgli began to feel dizzy.

"First Kaa will put the monkeys
under his spell," said Bagheera.

Baloo put his big furry arms around
Mowgli.

He squeezed Mowgli hard.

"Then Kaa will give the monkeys
a terrible hug," said Baloo.

"Oooh," said Mowgli. "I will stay
far, far away from Kaa."

But Kaa was looking for Mowgli.
And that afternoon he found him.
Mowgli was swimming in the river.
He floated with his eyes closed.
He did not see Kaa hiding in the grass.

Bagheera and Baloo were asleep.
They did not see Kaa either.

Quietly, ever so quietly, Kaa slid into the water.

When Mowgli opened his eyes, he was looking right at Kaa!

Kaa's head waved back and forth.

"You are under my s-s-spell," said Kaa.

Mowgli began to feel dizzy.

Then Baloo woke up.
He saw Kaa with Mowgli.
Baloo rushed into the water.

"Scram, Kaa!" Baloo shouted. "Mowgli is not going to be your dinner today!"

Kaa slithered away.

"Next time I will be more s-s-sneaky,"
said Kaa. "I will get that boy s-s-soon."

"You will have to be more careful,"
Baloo and Bagheera said to Mowgli.
Mowgli did not like to be scolded.
"I am not afraid of Kaa," he thought.

So the next day Mowgli went for a walk—all by himself.

By and by he heard a lot of noise.

He stopped to listen.

"What is happening?" Mowgli wondered. "I will go see."

Mowgli came to a tree full of monkeys.
Under the tree was a hunter's trap.
And inside the trap was Kaa!
The monkeys were yelling and laughing
at Kaa.

"Those monkeys are brave because
I am trapped," said Kaa to the boy.

"What will happen to you?" asked Mowgli.

"It is Kaa's turn to be s-s-somebody's
dinner," Kaa said sadly.

"I can help you," said Mowgli.
He lifted the latch on the trap.
Then he opened the door.

Out came Kaa!

"I am grateful," said Kaa to Mowgli. "But I am also hungry. If I s-s-stay here, I will forget that you s-s-saved me."

Kaa slithered away.

Now all the monkeys
began to shout.

"Mowgli is a dummy!
He let the snake go free!"

"Let's get Mowgli!" cried
one of the monkeys.

"I am not afraid of
you silly monkeys!"
said Mowgli.

But Mowgli spoke too soon.

A monkey reached down out of
the tree and grabbed him.

"Help!" cried Mowgli.

Now he WAS afraid.

One monkey grabbed Mowgli's foot.
Another monkey grabbed Mowgli's arm.
They swung off through the trees—
holding on to the boy.
They did not see Kaa watching
from the grass.

At last the monkeys came to Monkey City.
They took Mowgli to their king.
"Here he is, O King!" they cried.

"Well, well," the monkey king
said to Mowgli. "How would you
like to live with us? We are
the best animals in the jungle."

"We are handsome!"

"We are strong!"

"We are very,
very wise!"

"No, thanks!" said Mowgli.
"You are just a lot of
silly old monkeys."

The monkeys did not like to be called silly old monkeys.

They picked up Mowgli and threw him into an old stone pit!

Now Mowgli was trapped!
There was no way out of the pit.
The sides were too high to climb.
Mowgli had to sit there and listen
to the monkeys laughing.

Suddenly the monkeys stopped laughing.

Mowgli wondered why.

Kaa the python had
come to Monkey City!
The monkeys ran
from him.

Kaa looked down into
the old stone pit.
   Mowgli looked up at Kaa.
   Mowgli knew he could
not escape from Kaa.
   Not this time.
   Baloo and Bagheera
were far, far away.

Kaa's tail began to drop down into the pit.

Now Mowgli was REALLY afraid.

He remembered Kaa's terrible hug.

But Kaa did not hug Mowgli!
He twisted his body into
steps.
Slowly Mowgli climbed out of
the pit.

When Mowgli reached the top,
he was face to face with Kaa.
"Are you . . . are you going
to eat me?" asked Mowgli.
"Not at all," said Kaa.
"You s-s-saved my life. Now I
will s-s-save yours."

While Kaa kept
the monkeys up in
their tree, Mowgli
walked away.

He walked out of Monkey City.

Then he ran through the jungle
to find his friends.

Mowgli was glad to be safe with
Bagheera and Baloo again.

It was a long time before he went
for another walk by himself.

Mowgli knew that Kaa would soon
be after him again.

But he would always remember the day
that his enemy had been his friend.